Aunt Nancy's
Three Rules for Life:

Read
Exercise
& Be Nice

Written by Nancy K. Roberson

Illustrated by Danilo Cerovic

gatekeeper press™

Aunt Nancy's Three Rules for Life: Read, Exercise, and Be Nice

Published by Gatekeeper Press

2167 Stringtown Rd, Suite 109

Columbus, OH 43123-2989

www.GatekeeperPress.com

Library of Congress Control Number: 2021930196

ISBN (hardcover): 9781662908149

ISBN (paperback): 9781662908156

eISBN: 9781662908163

Dedicated to Aunt Nancy's great nieces and nephews showcased in this book. Thanks to their Moms and Dads for raising caring children who have made my life more complete. I love all of you dearly.

Hailey   Ethan   Phoebe   Emma
Andrew   Jake   Mason
Adam   Alex   Gigi   Ben

Dear kids,

I want each of you to remember these three things.

They are Aunt Nancy's Three Rules for Life:

"Read, Exercise, and Be Nice"!

When I see you next time, I hope each of you can tell me how you have practiced them.

"Hi Aunt Nancy! I remember the three things," says Ethan!

"What are they?" asks Aunt Nancy.

"Read, Exercise, and Be Nice!" says Ethan.

Hailey asks, "Why are they so important to remember?"

Aunt Nancy explains, "If you do these three things every day, 'Read, Exercise, and Be Nice', you'll become a smarter, healthier, and better person! Your parents and I will also be very proud of you!"

"Today you are going to learn something new, snow skiing. What important 'thing' are we doing today?" asks Aunt Nancy.

The kids all yell, "Exercising!"

On Aunt Nancy's next visit with Emma, she goes inside and asks, "Hi Emma, what are you doing?"

Emma says, "I'm reading! I love to read nature books."

"Why?" asks Aunt Nancy.

"It is fun and I learn new things," says Emma.

Andrew says to his two brothers, Adam and Alex, "Come with me, I will pull you two in the wagon. Let's have some fun! I want to tell Aunt Nancy next time we see her that I can be nice *and* exercise at the same time!"

Aunt Nancy greets the family, "Hi kids! It's great to visit you again!"

"I can carry your suitcase for you," said Ethan.

"Thank you, Ethan. That is very nice!" says Aunt Nancy. "Do you remember the three things, 'Read, Exercise, and Be Nice'? We can go to the Pumpkin Patch later today for our 'exercise'."

"Aren't all the pumpkins beautiful?" says Aunt Nancy.

Phoebe turns to Jake and says in a nice voice, "Jake, today we are going to get some exercise and see all the pumpkins. Please hold my hand, I don't want you to fall."

Jake yells, "Hey! I can be nice too," and goes outside to feed the cat and dog.

Andrew, Adam, and Alex are returning from a car ride with their parents. During the trip, they played a game of "How Many Road Signs Can You Read?" Andrew is thinking about Aunt Nancy's Three Rules for Life: Read, Exercise, and Be Nice! and says, "We can tell Aunt Nancy we could read all the road signs!"

Aunt Nancy says, "I'm so happy to see you again! Since we are all together today, we are going swimming at the Lake to have fun and exercise!"

The kids all yell, "Yay! We can bring our own goggles and floaties! We can't wait!"

While Aunt Nancy is visiting, she also goes to see Emma, Mason, and Ben all practicing soccer with each other. While she is having so much fun watching them play soccer, the kids are getting lots of fun exercise!

Going to Scouts day camp is teaching Mason and Ben to always use good manners, even when having fun. So everyone can enjoy roasting marshmallows to make s'mores, Mason collects wood and Ben builds a fire.

Ben says, "By helping prepare the fire, we are being nice and getting exercise too!"

All the kids realize how important it is to do these three things every day, "Read, Exercise, and Be Nice." They send Aunt Nancy pictures every time they learn new ways to practice these three things. They know this makes Aunt Nancy very happy and also makes them smarter, healthier, and better people!

Aunt Nancy asks YOU, "Do you remember the three important things? What are they? 'Read, Exercise and Be Nice'! Have YOU done them today?"

Nancy Roberson's first professional job was a junior high school teacher. However, she spent most of her career in the educational publishing sector where she served in key leadership and management roles at major companies. She also served as President of the Board of Directors for Teach My Kid to Read through February 2021, a nonprofit startup with a mission to provide parents, librarians, educators, and anyone interested in literacy education with the tools and resources to help all kids learn to read. Nancy established her "Three Rules for Life" many years ago as she wanted to teach her young great nieces and nephews about the importance of doing these "three things" every day. To this day, they all know and do the "three things"!

Nancy holds a Bachelor of Science degree from the University of Arkansas and a Master's degree in Education from the University of Tulsa.